Little Philippe Of Belgium

Madeline Brandeis

Edition : Culturea (Hérault, 34)
Contact : infos@culturea.fr
Print in Germany by Books on Demand
Design and layout : Derek Murphy
Layout : Reedsy (https://reedsy.com/)
ISBN : 9791041819720
Légal deposit : July 2023

Little Philippe Of Belgium

Chapter I

THE BRUSSELS SPROUT

The Brussels Sprout sat among the cabbages, thinking.

The Brussels Sprout was not a little vegetable. He was a little boy. His name was really Philippe. But he was called "Petit Choux de Bruxelles" (pe-tē´ shōō de brük-sel), which means in French, "Little Brussels Sprout." French is spoken in Brussels, and this little boy was born in that city.

But he now lived on a farm a few miles outside of Brussels.

The name "choux" (shōō) or "cabbage," is often used as a pet name. That was the reason why Philippe's parents called him Little Cabbage or Sprout.

Sprout was a very good name for this little boy, because new ideas were always sprouting in his head.

He was always dreaming dreams and wishing wishes. He was never satisfied.

One of his dearest wishes was for a little sister.

Today he sat among the cabbages and thought deeply. He was wondering why one of the cabbages did not open and give him a baby sister.

This may sound queer to you. But Philippe was only five years old, and he believed very earnestly that babies pop out of cabbages.

It is a Belgian folk tale. Philippe had planted these cabbages in his garden for this very purpose.

But no baby sister had popped out of a cabbage yet.

Philippe wanted a baby sister with whom to play. He was the kind of little boy who always longed for something.

He was not really discontented. But he liked new things to happen. And besides he was a bit lonely on that farm, with nobody to play with him.

"Why do you look so sad today, my little cabbage?" asked his mother.

She had just come out of the house and stood looking down at him.

"I am thinking that never will the baby, Cauliflower, come!" he answered.

Cauliflower was what Philippe had determined to name the sister for whom he longed. Cauliflower in French is "choux fleur" (shōō-flûr), which means "cabbage flower."

"Are you quite certain that none of the cabbages moved today?" asked Mother Yvelle (ē-věl'), smiling strangely.

Philippe shook his head and replied, "They are all quite still, Mamma. The little sister is not coming."

Then Mother Yvelle laughed and threw both arms about her little boy.

"Do not say that," she cried.

Philippe looked at her and saw a shiny light in her eyes. Mother Yvelle said softly, "Soon—soon—the great day is coming when my Philippe shall be a little brother!"

A little brother! Philippe could hardly believe the words that Mother Yvelle had spoken. But it was true. Mother Yvelle spoke only the truth.

When Mother Yvelle went into the house, Philippe looked at each cabbage carefully.

"Which one will it be?" he wondered excitedly. "Which cabbage will open and give me my little Cauliflower?"

Philippe was happy beyond all dreams. He examined each vegetable. But he could find no sign of the coming baby in any of them.

He went to the barn. There he spoke to the big dogs, his only companions. He told them the great news.

These dogs did not have much time to play with a little boy. They were usually working. For Belgian dogs draw carts for their owners.

Philippe's mother had a big vegetable cart. Nearly every morning she loaded it with peas and beans and carrots and onions. She then hitched the dogs and drove them to the market place in Brussels. Here she would sit at a stand and sell her fresh vegetables.

Philippe usually went with her. But sometimes he stayed at home with the gardener.

Philippe's father was a chef. Papa Paul was a very fine chef and could cook some of the best French and Belgian dishes.

He cooked in a fine restaurant in Brussels. He came home late at night, and so Philippe saw little of his father.

But he admired his father very much. He wanted to cook the way his father did some day. That was another great desire in the heart of this little boy. Philippe dreamed of some day becoming a chef like his father.

But he did not look like Papa Paul. Philippe's father was stout and round and smiling. And Philippe was rather slender, and had a serious little face with big dreamy eyes. He was like his mother.

Mother Yvelle was thin and pale and sad-looking.

You see, she and her husband had lived through the terrible World War.

There are, however, people whose dispositions are so jolly that they forget sadness. Philippe's father was one of these people. Though Papa Paul wore a wooden leg, it did not seem to affect his sunny smile. When he was in the war he had been shot in the leg, and now he wore a leg of wood. He had been a chef only since the war.

Before the war Philippe's parents had farmed and raised vegetables together. They had been happy farmers. But their farm had been blown to bits by the enemy.

Many stormy years passed, and many terrible things happened to these poor people. But finally the sunny smile won out. Here was Papa Paul cooking in one of the best restaurants in Belgium, while Mother Yvelle was the farmer.

Mother Yvelle looked forward to the day when Philippe should be old enough to help her drive the dogs to town with the vegetables.

Philippe, too, wanted that day to come. He wanted to drive the fine dogs to town.

From the barn he made his way to a tiny shack, which was his own little kitchen. Here he spent many hours over a small stove his father had made for him. He prepared dishes that he thought were very fine.

Today he had gathered some vegetables and carried them with the other things he had in his arms.

"What are you going to cook today?" asked the gardener, Emile (ā-mēl′).

He stood in the door holding a big rake and looking amused.

"A stew—a very fine stew," answered Philippe, and he began to pour a number of things into a pot.

"What are you putting into the stew?" asked Emile.

"Onions and peas, some rice, a nice little fat snail and a root," the boy replied, as he began to stir.

"A root? What kind of a root?" inquired the gardener.

"Oh, a root that I found. A very big one. I dug it up."

Emile laughed and moved on. One could never tell what went into Philippe's stews. Sometimes Emile was made to taste them. Then he had to tell Philippe that the stews were good. But Emile always had to drink some water afterwards to wash away the taste.

But then Philippe was such a little boy. Besides, the gardener felt sorry for him, because he was lonesome.

Philippe called the gardener Emile Epinard (ā-mēl´ ā-pē-när´), which means "Emile Spinach." And, indeed, Emile did look like a ragged leaf of spinach!

Philippe had a vegetable game. He always tried to think what vegetable each person looked like.

Then he would call that person by the name of that vegetable. It was fun.

For instance, he always called his father "Papa Pomme" (pōm), which means "Father Apple." This name rather shocked Mother Yvelle. But it pleased the jolly round chef. He would tell his friends about it and laugh until his fat sides shook.

Philippe had a friend whom he called "String Bean Simon," another, "Celery Susan," and many others he gave different nicknames of the same kind.

As he was stirring his mixture, he suddenly remembered that he had not told Emile the great news.

"Oh, Emile Spinach, Emile Spinach," he called, "did you know that soon, soon the little sister will be here?"

But Emile Spinach had gone into the fields.

"This stew will be for the baby, Cauliflower," thought Philippe. "She will like this stew."

Soon he heard his mother's voice calling from the house, "Supper, my little one. Come to supper."

Carrying his precious pot, he started toward the cottage. On the way he once more examined the cabbages.

But there was still no sign of a baby in any of them.

As he neared the house, he noticed a beautiful rose growing near the wall.

It had been in full bloom the day before. Now it was beginning to droop. Philippe looked at it pityingly.

"Poor rose!" he said. "Tomorrow you will be dead."

Then he went into the house.

The next morning Philippe arose early. He ran to the cabbage patch. But the cabbages all looked neat and whole. None had been disturbed during the night.

"She has not come!" moaned poor Philippe.

Sadly he started toward the cottage, when again he noticed the rose. But this time it was only the stem he saw. The petals all had fallen to the ground.

"Poor rose!" he sighed. "She is dead!"

There was a step behind him. A heavy hand was laid on his shoulder.

His father's deep, fine voice boomed, "What are you saying, my little cabbage?"

"Poor rose is dead!" answered Philippe sadly.

"What!" exclaimed Papa Pomme. "Why, Baby Rose is born!"

"Baby Rose?" questioned Philippe.

"Yes, my son," Papa Pomme said. "Your little sister came to us last night—your little sister Rose."

Philippe leaped up and threw his arms about his father's neck in a burst of joy. At last his little sister was here! Then he looked at the dead rose, and from it, to the live and healthy cabbages. He smiled knowingly.

"Papa Pomme," he said, "it was not from the cabbage that Baby came. So, you see, she shall not be our Cauliflower. It was the rose that opened to give her to us. That is why she is our Baby Rose."

Chapter II

PAPA POMME'S SURPRISE

For over a year now Philippe, the little Brussels Sprout, had been going to the market place with Emile Spinach. Mother had to stay at home with Baby Rose.

Philippe felt himself almost a man now. If only Emile would stay at home and let him drive the dogs alone! Ah, that would be heaven, indeed. Another dream was to bring his precious Baby Rose to the market place some day. Philippe was always wishing wishes.

Rose was so tiny. At first she could only laugh at Philippe's happy face as he bent over her cradle. She pulled his hair or clutched his finger.

Now she could stand alone and say a word or two. She was beautiful. She was fair and dainty, and her eyes were as blue as a summer sky. How Philippe loved his Baby Rose!

Soon Mother had promised to bring her to the market place. What a proud boy Philippe would be when he might set her upon the low cart on top of the vegetables and drive her to town! The fine, sleek dogs would be proud, too, knowing that a rare flower rested upon their vegetable load.

Philippe had a sweet voice and sang a number of Belgian folk songs. He was beginning to teach his Rose a little vegetable song which he had made up.

He had a fine plan. He wanted to station Rose in the market place, and have her sing for the passers-by. How proud the little fellow was of his baby sister!

Today as he walked along beside the sturdy dogs, he sang gayly. He was happier than usual. Today an exciting thing was to happen. Papa Pomme had told him that he would call at the market place and take him to lunch. Papa Pomme did not often do this. But today he was given the afternoon to himself.

Papa had put his finger to his lips and said mysteriously to Philippe, "You shall dine with me, little one; and then, in the afternoon—ah, you shall see!"

So as Philippe walked along, he wondered what surprise his father had planned for the afternoon. When he reached the market place, or Grande Place (grän pläs), as it is called in French, he helped Emile Spinach unload the vegetables. Many other farmers were arranging their wares. Some sold beautiful flowers, and others sold fruits. There were portions of the square set aside for sellers of birds and dogs and all manner of different articles.

The Grande Place in Brussels is one of the most beautiful places of its kind in the world. There stands the city hall, built half a century before America was discovered. There are many other beautiful, gilded buildings. The Grande Place in Brussels shines in the splendor of past glory.

Here sat the little boy, Philippe, and helped sell his mother's vegetables. He often glanced at the clock and hoped his father would not be late. He wanted to know what Papa Pomme was planning for the afternoon.

Papa Pomme was on time. He took his son by the hand. They made their way to a restaurant, where little tables were placed out on the sidewalk.

Here people sat in leisurely style, eating hearty dinners. The jolly-faced chef and his little son settled themselves at a corner table. The menu before them was indeed tempting.

Although Philippe was anxious to know his father's surprise, he could not allow it to stand in the way of his appetite. How could any boy do that?

Belgian food is tempting to everyone. It is as dainty as the French food. It is as wholesome as the Dutch. And it has something about it that is neither French nor Dutch, but purely Belgian.

Perhaps the reason lies in the fact that Belgium is so small. It is a matter of only a few hours for vegetables and fruits to travel from a distant farm to a Brussels table. Therefore, all food is fresh.

Papa Pomme ordered "potage," the famous thick soup, dear to all the French and Belgians. Then they had a roast, and for dessert, strawberries and a huge plate of gingerbread. Belgian strawberries and gingerbread are very famous and are said to be the best in the world.

While they ate, they did not talk. Eating was a serious matter with Papa Pomme and Philippe.

So absorbed did Philippe become that he forgot his manners. He reached across the table and pulled toward him the long loaf of French bread.

"Ho, ho!" cried Papa Pomme. "Not so fast! Come! Do you not use your tongue when you want something which is beyond your reach?"

Philippe blushed. Then he replied stoutly, "Yes, Papa Pomme; but my arm is much longer than my tongue!"

Papa Pomme laughed and gained another pound. Philippe went on eating happily.

When they left the restaurant they walked down the street together.

"Papa Pomme, where are you taking me?" asked Philippe, puzzled.

For Papa Pomme was acting in a very mysterious way.

"Do not ask yet!" he said. "Soon you shall see."

Soon Philippe did see. For they stopped in front of a big theater. In Europe a motion picture theater is called a cinema.

"Now, little Philippe," laughed Papa Pomme, "you know my surprise!"

Philippe threw his cap in the air and shouted, "Hooray! The cinema!"

It was a special treat to the little boy to be taken to the cinema! He had been to one only once before in his life.

They were to see a great film today. It was the story of the World War and the part that little Belgium had played. It showed how the enemy had started to march through Belgium in order to reach Paris. It showed how the loyal Belgians and their brave King Albert had helped the Allies to win their victory by stopping that march.

Long ago a treaty had been made which said that no nation should take an army through Belgium to attack another nation. If ever such a thing happened, it was Belgium's duty to stop them. In the year 1914, an enemy did try to go through her land. Belgium might have neglected her duty. She might have remained quiet and allowed the enemy to pass. Had she done this, she would never have been destroyed as she was. The enemy would have marched quietly through and left Belgium to its peaceful life.

The film showed how the Belgians fought. Still Belgium could not hold out against so powerful an enemy. At last she was conquered. But when that time came, the French were ready, and so were the English. So Paris was saved.

The audience shouted and clapped. But after that came sighs. The film showed how pitiful and sad was this poor little Belgium after the war.

That film left in the heart of Philippe a new dream. It was that film which was really the cause of the little boy's later adventures.

Chapter III

A NEIGHBOR

Five years passed. Philippe was now a tall boy of eleven. He was still called Sprout, and he was still full of wishing dreams and dreaming wishes.

But those dreams and wishes had changed since the time when he had longed for a baby sister. Of course, he never stopped being glad about Rose. She was the dearest little sister that a boy could have.

Philippe's desire to be a cook had disappeared. He had changed since that day when Papa Pomme had taken him to the cinema. For Philippe never forgot the film he had seen.

Philippe never forgot those terrible battle scenes. Often his eyes would fill with tears at the thought of the sad struggle and the bravery of his little country.

The boy who had once dreamed of vegetables now had other dreams. The little boy, who had wanted some day to be a chef, now longed to become a great hero like his own country's king. He longed to do a great deed himself and to have adventures. But all he could do was to sell vegetables.

No, that was not all. Now he could read about his country. And he did. Philippe read and read. Every book he could find he devoured. Stories of Belgium's cities and people Philippe learned and loved. Tales of wonder kept him interested for hours.

"If only I might travel and have adventures!" sighed the little vegetable boy.

He was now old enough to drive the dog-cart to market alone. He went each day, with Baby Rose perched on top of the vegetables, laughing and gurgling with joy.

All the way to town Philippe sang with his little sister. When they reached the Grande Place, he set the baby upon the counter. Then the little girl, with her golden curls and her sunny smile, and the tall, handsome boy, with his wavy hair and his dreamy eyes, sang and attracted many people to the booth. It did not take them long to sell their vegetables.

Now as Philippe unloaded his produce, he did not know that today something unusual was going to happen. Rose fluttered about and filled the dogs' drinking bowl. All dog-carts in Belgium carry drinking bowls, and a bit of carpet for the animals to lie down upon. Rose filled the bowl, and the huge beasts licked her hands with gratitude.

There was a new member of the dog family who had come to town with them today. It was Trompke (trŏmp'-ky). Trompke was a puppy. He did not work. He was Philippe's own puppy.

"Trompke" means "tambourine" in Brussels French. The puppy was thus named because he had such a fat little round tummy.

Trompke loved Philippe. Today was the first time he had been allowed to follow the cart to town. He was wild with excitement.

"Stop barking, Trompke!" commanded Philippe, as he arranged the vegetables on the stand.

"Lie down, Tum-Tum," cried Baby Rose.

And Trompke lay at the baby's feet.

Just then Philippe noticed some one in the booth next to their own. A tall man was moving about arranging vegetables. This booth had not been used for a very long time.

"Now," thought Philippe, "we shall have a neighbor."

Philippe smiled at the man, who was staring at the two children. Then the man looked down at the puppy, which was whining unhappily at Philippe's feet.

"Keep him quiet," said the man angrily.

Philippe answered, "He means no harm. He is only excited. It's his first trip to town."

The man did not answer but turned toward his vegetables. Philippe was puzzled. He had never before met anyone like his neighbor.

The man wore ragged clothes, and his face was sunburned. His eyes were coal black and seemed to flash fire. He had a wild look about him. He was tall and moved like a cat.

Suddenly he leaned over toward Philippe.

"Keep that dog quiet, will you?" he snarled.

Trompke was still whining softly, though he could hardly be heard.

"He does no harm," answered Philippe.

The man's flashing eyes gleamed as he replied, "He keeps the people away. Nobody has come to buy at the booths yet. It is the fault of that dog."

Philippe could only smile at such stupidity. To think that a little whining dog could keep people away! But the man seemed nervous.

So Philippe said, "Just wait, sir. I will have the crowds here in a short time. Come, Rose; let us sing!"

Little Rose stood upon the counter. She looked like a big doll. Her golden curls shone in the sunlight. Philippe stood by her side, and together they sang in voices clear and sweet. They sang the little nonsense song that Philippe had made up for his sister. It ran:

"I wouldn't be an artichoke,

And have my heart torn out,

I wouldn't be a lettuce,

With my head thrown all about,

I'd hate to be a cornstalk,

For folk my ears would pull;

Potatoes must feel dreadful

'Cause with dirt their eyes are full."

A few people began to wander over to the vegetable booth. They stood and watched the two children. They smiled at the quaint little vegetable boy, and looked admiringly at the pretty baby. Then the children began their second stanza, as more and more people gathered around the booth.

"It must be hard for spinach, too;

His leaves are never read;

Poor mushroom, with the fairy folk

All sitting on his head!

Old Mr. Onion grieves so much.

He makes us all boohoo!

I'm glad I'm not a vegetable,

But just a child. Aren't you?"

Many people had now crowded round and some began to buy vegetables. Philippe was kept busy serving them. Baby Rose smiled and dimpled at everyone. She sang other songs that Philippe had made up. Then she sang "The Brabançonne" (brä-bän-sōn'), Belgium's national anthem.

The vegetables were slowly disappearing. But from the booth next door, not a vegetable was bought. Philippe cast a look in the direction of the tall dark man, who was standing with his arms folded.

Philippe looked down at the man's vegetables. For the first time he noticed that they were not fresh. They were wilted and stale.

"It is no wonder the people do not buy," thought Philippe.

But he felt sorry, nevertheless. When the crowd had left, and the selling was over, he turned to the man.

"I am sorry," he said. "But— —"

Philippe was going to tell him that people will not buy stale vegetables. But the man interrupted him.

"Thank you, but I do not need your advice," he said.

Philippe watched him as he began to throw his vegetables into a barrel and prepare to leave. He whistled as he did so.

Philippe lifted Rose from the counter and they, too, made preparations for departure.

All the way home, the boy seemed to see before him that stranger's face.

When the children reached home, a surprise awaited them.

"Papa Pomme is home! Hurrah!" cried Philippe.

Sometimes Papa Pomme came home to dinner, and that was a great treat. But this evening Papa Pomme looked grave. He began to talk with Mother Yvelle. Philippe listened.

"They say that this thief has stolen from several farms about here," said Papa Pomme. "You had better warn Emile to watch."

"A thief, Papa?" asked Philippe, whose eyes were very big.

"Yes, my boy," Papa Pomme replied. "A man who goes about at night stealing vegetables from people's farms—a vegetable thief. I wish they could catch him. It is very hard for the poor farmers to have their produce stolen. This thief is a wicked man."

Philippe suddenly thought of his dark neighbor in the market place. Could it be— —? Oh, no.

Still there were those stale vegetables. But Philippe refused to think of such a thing.

"Papa," he asked, "if this thief is caught, what will they do with him?"

"They will put him in prison, my son," answered Papa Pomme.

Chapter IV

ZELIE

Philippe did not know how nearly right he had been. He had wondered whether his neighbor in the market place could be the thief.

But Philippe did not like to think evil of people, so he drove away that thought. But the tall dark man was really the vegetable thief.

Next day when Philippe arrived at the Grande Place, he looked for his neighbor. Yes, there was the man with another load of stale vegetables. He was piling them upon his counter.

Today Philippe noticed that there was a little girl with him. She was helping him spread out the wilted vegetables. Philippe did not know that during the night this evil man had stolen those vegetables from a poor farmer.

He had stolen them and now he had brought them to the market place to sell. They were not fresh like Philippe's vegetables, because the thief did not know how to take care of them.

The little girl with Philippe's neighbor glanced shyly at the boy. She was dark like the man. But her face was not like his. It was sweet and pretty.

Suddenly Philippe was surprised to hear the man call out cheerily: "Good morning to you, friend, and to the little golden-haired singing bird."

The man had changed from the day before. Philippe now rather liked his weather-beaten face. It was all wrinkled with smiles.

"Good morning to you, sir," answered Philippe.

"This is Zelie, my little daughter," said the fellow, still smiling. "Zelie, go over and shake hands with the boy and with the little singing bird. You must get acquainted."

Zelie obeyed. She seemed a shy but pleasant little girl. She was a year or so younger than Philippe. Her black hair hung straight from under a gypsy-like bandanna. She wore earrings in her ears. Her eyes were black, but they did not flash. They smiled at Philippe.

The two children talked. Philippe found Zelie bright and interesting. She had traveled a great deal. She spoke of her travels about the country.

While the morning passed, the two children became friends.

As before, the boy and his sister sold their fresh fine vegetables. People gathered around their booth and clapped for their singing. But nobody stopped to buy from the man beside them.

Still, instead of being jealous of Philippe, the stranger kept smiling at his neighbor. When the crowd had gone and it was time to start for home, the man came over to Philippe's booth.

"Did my Zelie tell you of her travels?" he asked Philippe.

"Oh, yes," replied the boy eagerly. "What great fortune to be able to wander about the country as you do, sir!"

The man looked at Philippe with those flashing eyes.

Then he said, "You could do so, too. You and the singing bird could earn great sums of money wandering about and singing. Why not go?"

Philippe started. Such a thing had never entered his mind. Though he had dreamed of adventure and travel, it had been only a dream.

"Oh, I couldn't, sir," he answered. "My mother would not let me go."

"Ha, ha!" laughed the man good-naturedly. "It would not be hard to persuade her. Tell her that Zelie and I will take you with us and you will be as safe and comfortable as you are at home."

Philippe wrinkled his brow. Then he began to prepare to go home. Somehow, this plan was a little startling. Still, it did tempt him.

He seemed to like the man much better today. Zelie, too, was a splendid companion. All the way home Philippe thought hard.

As the days passed, he grew to like Zelie and her father more and more. Zelie showed Philippe many delightful souvenirs from many parts of Belgium. She had also journeyed to other countries and spoke of those lands.

She was always sweet and happy. But Philippe sometimes wondered why there was a frightened look in her eyes. That frightened look came when she was with her father. She seemed to lose it when she sat talking with Philippe.

The man, whose name was Tom, asked Philippe one day, "Will you teach Zelie to sing your songs? They are so clever and bright."

"Certainly, sir," promised Philippe.

So he taught Zelie all of the little songs that he and Rose sang.

Today the sun was shining in the market place, and birds were singing. Philippe felt full of gladness. He met Zelie and her father, who had a smile on his face.

"What a fine day for traveling!" he cried. "How I should like to start out and wander to far places!"

Tom's sly eyes beamed. He slapped Philippe on the back lightly.

"That is just what Zelie and I are planning," he said. "Tomorrow we leave. Why could not you and the singing bird go with us?

"We shall go to every part of Belgium and take along our big organ. Zelie will play the organ, while you and Baby Rose sing."

Philippe's heart pounded. Yes, why not? He looked at Zelie. He thought she must be delighted. But he was amazed to see a look of fear in her little dark face.

"What luck!" he cried. "Are you not pleased, Zelie?"

"If you would come it might be jolly," the girl answered.

"Why not?" again thought Philippe. He said, "I'll ask my mother and father tonight. I shall tell you in the morning."

"Good!" Tom smiled. "Zelie and I can wait until the following day to start our journey. Then we four shall set out together."

That night Philippe asked his parents if he might go traveling with Tom and Zelie.

"This is a strange man," said Papa Pomme. "How do you know that he may not be a wicked man? Besides, a wandering life is a hard one, and Baby Rose is too young."

"But I am old and strong, Papa Pomme," begged Philippe. "I shall make great sums of money, too. Do, do let me go."

"Not yet, little cabbage," said Papa Pomme.

Philippe's dream was shattered. He cried himself to sleep that night.

The next day in the market place Tom met the children with an eager question.

"Well? Do we start tomorrow?" he asked.

"My father will not let me go," Philippe said.

The man scowled.

"Foolish," he frowned, "foolish! It would bring you money, and you could make your parents rich."

Philippe scowled, too.

"Yes," he agreed, "I told my father. But still he refuses to allow me to go."

"It is too bad," the man said. He shrugged his shoulders. "But Zelie and I must leave tomorrow. And maybe some day you will decide to join us."

Philippe wondered what Tom meant.

"You know you are a big boy now," Tom continued. "It is a shame for you to waste your time sitting in a market place selling vegetables."

He winked at Philippe slyly, and then started to whistle. Oh, how lucky was this Tom, thought Philippe; and the little girl, Zelie, too! But still Philippe noticed that Zelie's eyes were sad.

Chapter V

NEW FRIENDS

Philippe lay in bed and thought of Tom and of Zelie. Yes, mostly he thought of Zelie. He would never see her again. Tom was taking her away in the morning. What a pity!

She was the most interesting little friend the boy had ever had. Now he would be lonely again. Rose was still so young.

Of course, he had his books. But he did so long to wander through the country. It was summer time, and there was no school. Oh, happy Zelie!

"But was she really happy?" Philippe wondered.

She had once told him that she had to push the big organ about while they begged their way.

It was a heavy thing, that organ, and Philippe had asked, "Doesn't it tire you, Zelie?"

Zelie had looked quickly at her father and had caught Tom's gleaming eye.

"No," she had replied, "it is fun."

Philippe had envied her. If he might go along, he could push the organ for her. He was strong. And he might help Tom, too.

Philippe did not know what his friend Tom was doing just at this moment. As Philippe lay in his comfortable little bed, he did not know that Tom was stealing his father's vegetables. Philippe did not know that poor Zelie was right under the window with Tom, helping to steal Papa Pomme's vegetables.

The next morning Emile Spinach ran into the house, very much excited.

"The vegetable thief has been in the garden, sir!" he cried to Papa Pomme.

Sure enough, their little farm had been robbed.

When Philippe and Rose arrived at the market place, the booth next to theirs was empty.

Of course Philippe never dreamed that Tom was the thief. He missed his neighbors sadly. He pictured them pushing along the organ and playing in market places all over Belgium. He thought of them strolling along the pleasant roads.

He could hear Tom's gay whistle. He could see Zelie's little dark face. He wondered whether Zelie would sing the songs he had taught her. She had a pretty voice. She was not so small and cunning as Baby Rose, but she had a charm of her own.

Philippe became discontented. He sometimes wandered about the streets instead of staying in the market place. Of course, he only did this when Emile Spinach was there to stay with Rose.

Philippe was quieter than usual.

Papa Pomme said one day to Mother Yvelle, "I am worried about the boy. He is different. Something bothers him."

Papa Pomme did worry about Philippe. Papa Pomme worried so much that once he put sugar in the soup and salt in the pastry. The manager of the restaurant scolded Papa Pomme.

One day Philippe was walking toward his father's restaurant. As he approached, a taxicab drove up and stopped a few doors away. Two gentlemen stepped out.

Philippe smiled as he heard one of the gentlemen ask the taxi driver, "Can you direct us to a restaurant?"

The gentleman had a very funny French accent. He continued, "We have heard so much about this delicious Belgian food. We are very hungry."

The taxi driver must have been hungry, too. He evidently wanted to be off to his own lunch.

For he replied sharply, "There are many restaurants. Just walk along any street. They can always be smelled!"

The unobliging taxi driver laughed at his own stupid joke. Then he started his motor and was off.

The two gentlemen stood for a moment looking at each other. Then one said something in a language that Philippe did not understand. But he felt sure that it was English.

The little boy walked over to the gentlemen.

"Excuse me, sirs," he began in French. "I heard you asking for a place to eat. I can take you to the best restaurant in Brussels."

The gentlemen looked at the little Belgian boy standing before them. Then one of them smiled and said something in English to the other. Philippe did not understand the words, but if you had been there you would have heard the gentleman say to his friend, "Let us take his word for it. He may know something about food. Boys usually do."

The other one laughed and said in French to Philippe, "Thank you. We shall be glad to follow you."

Of course, Philippe led the gentlemen to his father's restaurant. He held the door open for them to enter, and started to leave.

But the gentleman who spoke French said, "Come! Wouldn't you like to lunch with us? You might tell us a bit about the art of Belgian eating. What do you say?"

"Thank you," said Philippe.

He could always eat. His dreams did not prevent that.

So the two foreign gentlemen and the little Belgian boy sat down to lunch. Philippe showed them how a Belgian orders a meal. They were amused at the child's knowledge of all these fine dishes. They asked him how he knew so much. Philippe then told them about Papa Pomme.

"Aha!" exclaimed the gentleman who spoke French. "It is a fine thing for a boy to have a papa who is a chef. Is it not?"

Philippe laughed and agreed. Then the same gentleman told about himself. He said, "My friend and I are touring through Belgium. My friend is an American. It is his first trip over here. I am from England. We are leaving tomorrow for Antwerp. Today we are going to see the sights of Brussels."

Philippe did full justice to the food spread before him. The men watched the hungry boy with great amusement.

The Englishman said, "Well, I must say you do eat well!"

Philippe stopped long enough to look up into his face and reply roguishly, "Yes, sir. I have been practicing all my life!"

The two gentlemen laughed. The Englishman had, of course, translated the words to his friend. They thought Philippe a very jolly lad. They did not know how really discontented he was. How little we can tell sometimes by looking at people what is really going on in their hearts!

"But now tell us," asked the Englishman. "Have you always lived in Brussels?"

"I have lived here all my life," Philippe answered. He then added timidly, "If you would like me to take you around the city after lunch I could show you many interesting sights. There are few places I do not know in Brussels."

"An excellent plan," cried the Englishman.

Then he told his friend, the American, what the Belgian boy had offered to do.

"Good!" said the American in English. "And I hope he knows as much about cities as he does about food. For then we shall find our minds stuffed as full as our stomachs!"

Chapter VI

PHILIPPE ACTS AS GUIDE

Philippe was a very good guide. He had learned much through his reading. Now he was able to show his new friends many interesting sights in Brussels. Also, he knew stories about all of them.

Brussels has been called "Paris in Little." This is because it is beautiful like Paris, with boulevards, similar buildings, and lovely parks. They passed avenues shaded by fine old lime trees. They admired statues and fountains all over the city.

Philippe led the two gentlemen to the palace of the King. The little Brussels boy pointed out a long stately building which stands just opposite a fine park.

"So this is the palace of good King Albert!" remarked the English gentleman. "He is considered a great ruler."

"He is," smiled Philippe, "and we love him."

Then the boy continued seriously, "But we Belgians and even King Albert do not like the idea of a kingdom."

"No?" inquired the Englishman, in a surprised tone.

"You know Englishmen are very true to their King."

"Yes, I have read in my books that they are," replied Philippe. "But we have good reasons for continuing with a monarchy. First, because of our love for King Albert, and then because we are afraid that without our kingdom we should split up. And you know that our motto is 'In union there is strength.'"

"But why do you fear being split up, as you say?" inquired the Englishman.

"Because," answered Philippe, "on one side of us is France, a republic; on the other side is Germany, also a republic. We Belgians are very close to both these countries because of many things. We are like them in many ways and we trade with them. We fear that without our King to hold us together we might become part of these countries. And we are very patriotic. We never want to be anything but Belgian!"

The little fellow stood and saluted the flag, which was flying from the palace.

"See! The flag!" said Philippe, pointing to the red, yellow, and black colors fluttering in the breeze. "I can tell you about that, also, if you would like me to do so."

"Certainly," replied the Englishman. Then he turned to his friend, the American, and said, "The little chap is just full of stories."

"That may be," replied the friend, "but I do not understand a word. It all sounds like Chinese to me!"

"Wait," laughed the Englishman. "I shall translate them to you later."

So Philippe told about his flag.

"The black in the flag is the King's color," said he. "It stands for constancy, wisdom, and prudence. The yellow stands for law and order. And red is for Belgium's liberty, fought for and obtained by the blood of her soldiers."

As they walked along the shady streets the English gentleman explained to his friend all that Philippe had said. The American nodded his head understandingly.

"That is very interesting," he said. "I do not blame the Belgians for being loyal to their King. They have good reasons."

"I am sure you would like to visit Waterloo," suggested Philippe. "I need not tell you the story of Waterloo," he smiled, "for everybody who has ever studied history knows about that."

But those who have not yet studied history may want to know that it is a famous battlefield where many wars were fought. The most famous of the battles was the struggle between the Duke of Wellington, who commanded the English army, and Napoleon Bonaparte who led the French.

When Philippe and his new friends had looked about for a while, the American gentleman remarked, "So this is where Napoleon met his Waterloo!"

It was here that Napoleon was conquered! That is why we still use the expression "met his Waterloo" when we mean to say "was defeated."

Philippe showed them the "Mound of the Lion," that great pyramid-shaped monument on the battlefield.

"It was built after the Battle of Waterloo, in memory of the Prince of Orange," he explained. "It is as large as a city block. The huge lion on the top is made of metal from captured French cannons. You know that the lion is the emblem of Belgium. The mound was built almost entirely by women who carried the dirt in pails."

Driving back to the city, the Englishman remarked, "It seems to me that tea time is approaching."

The little boy knew how important tea time is to Englishmen. So he suggested an excellent café where they might sit outside and watch the people.

While they were eating, Philippe explained to the Englishman how he loved to read. He told of his interest in the stories of his land.

"Then you do not want to be a chef some day like your father?" asked the gentleman.

Philippe shook his head.

"I want to do great things," he answered. "To travel, to have adventures."

The Englishman smiled.

"That is very natural," he remarked. He told his friend, the American, what the boy had said. His friend laughed.

"That sounds like an American boy," he said. "Ask him what he wants to do."

The Englishman asked Philippe this question.

The boy answered, "Oh, I should like to go to Antwerp (ănt´-w[~e]rp) and Ghent (gĕnt) and see the sights of Belgium, because I know so many stories about everything."

He then told them about his wandering friends, Tom and Zelie.

The Englishman remarked, "That is a hard life. It is much better to travel in a motor car." Then he smiled pleasantly and continued, "That is the way we travel. We are leaving for Antwerp tomorrow in our car."

Philippe's eyes shone. Here were more traveling folks. It seemed to the boy that everyone in the world was traveling except himself.

And while Philippe was thus thinking, the gentlemen were talking together in English.

Suddenly the Englishman turned to Philippe and asked, "How would you like to come along with us to Antwerp? You would make an excellent guide, since you know so much about the country."

Philippe's heart almost stopped beating.

"Oh, sir," he breathed, "that is very good of you." Then he hesitated. "But my father would not let me go."

"Where is your father?" asked the gentleman.

"At the restaurant where we lunched, sir. He is in the kitchen," replied Philippe.

"Very well; let us go and see him," suggested the Englishman.

Philippe led the gentlemen back to the restaurant. They followed him into the big kitchen.

There Philippe began to introduce them to Papa Pomme.

But the Englishman and Papa Pomme stared at one another and then they both cried out together, "Well, well, well!"

Philippe was surprised to see that Papa Pomme and this English gentleman already knew each other. They were very happy to meet again.

Papa Pomme turned to Philippe and said, "My boy, here you see a war-time friend of your father's. We were soldiers together in the World War. This gentleman was a great hero!"

The Englishman interrupted, "Oh, no, no, my friend, not so great a hero as you."

Then he looked at Papa Pomme's wooden leg and they both grew serious.

"But come! We have something to ask you," the gentleman suddenly observed. "My friend and I are going to Antwerp tomorrow. Will you allow your son to go along? We promise to take good care of him, and I'm sure he'll take splendid care of us. For you know, he has guided us through Brussels all day."

Papa Pomme fairly beamed with pride.

Then he said, "It is very kind of you, and I am delighted to have my Philippe go along with you. He has wanted so much to travel. Eh, little Philippe?"

And he pulled the boy's hair playfully.

"Oh, yes, Papa," joyfully agreed Philippe.

Papa Pomme continued, "And this time, I know that you will be safe, for you will be with an old friend of mine."

Philippe felt like dancing. What a wonderful thing had happened! He was really going on a trip. Of course, it was only to Antwerp, and then for just a few days. But even so, adventures might happen. Had Philippe known what adventure was really coming, he might not have been so happy.

Chapter VII

PHILIPPE RUNS AWAY

In the morning early a very excited little boy stood at the door of a farmhouse and gazed down the road.

Philippe was ready to travel to Antwerp with his friends, the two gentlemen. They had promised to stop by for him, and he had arisen early.

He was now in a state of great excitement. Mother Yvelle stood by his side. Her face was sad. She did not like to see her son leaving her. They heard a sound. The big motor car was approaching the tiny farm.

"Goodbye, Mamma. I shall be home soon. Do not worry," said Philippe.

He threw his arms about his mother's neck. The big car stopped before the door. The gentlemen jumped out.

"He will be back in two or three days," said the Englishman to Mother Yvelle. "We shall take good care of him. Have no fear."

Bundling Philippe into the car, the two gentlemen waved cheerily to the Belgian woman. She stood and watched them as they disappeared down the road.

"What is that?" cried the American, looking in surprise at his feet.

The lap robe of the car was moving.

"What can it be?" exclaimed the Englishman.

They lifted the lap robe. There, crouching on the floor of the car and looking up at them with friendly eyes, was Philippe's dog, Trompke.

"Trompke!" cried Philippe, "How did you get in? Shame!"

The puppy's tail went thump, thump! on the floor.

"Oh, I'm sorry," said Philippe. "I'll take him back if you'll stop the car."

"Never mind," laughed the Englishman. "Let him go along. He must have jumped in while we were saying goodbye to your mother."

"He would not let me go off without him," said Philippe. "He is so used to coming along."

So Trompke made the fourth traveler.

Along the smooth roads they motored. They passed tall poplar trees and well-tilled fields. They passed busy farmers. Everybody works in Belgium. It is an industrious little country.

They were soon in Antwerp. It is a short drive. They found the city less beautiful than Brussels. It seemed bristling with excitement and business. Some of the streets were picturesque and charming. Others were dirty and filled with rough people.

Philippe told his friend travelers that the most interesting place to see was the water front.

"It was there that the supplies, sent from your country during the World War, arrived," said the boy, looking at his American companion. "That is the port through which thousands and thousands of vessels pass each year."

They drove to the docks. Flags were flying from ships of almost every nation. There were miles and miles of masts and funnels. The air was full of busy noises.

"Did you know," asked the English gentleman, "that Antwerp is the second most important shipping port in Europe? Hamburg alone is more important."

After they had left the docks, they wandered about the city on foot.

They saw the house where the great painter, Rubens, lived.

It was growing late, and they talked of resting at a hotel before dinner. They were crossing a noisy street, on their way to a hotel, when Philippe suddenly saw Zelie and Tom.

The boy stopped. The two gentlemen were already on the opposite side. But Philippe stood stock still in the middle of the street and clutched his fat little puppy until the dog squealed. He had seen Zelie and Tom! But only for a moment.

Zelie was pushing the big organ. They had disappeared from sight, down an alleyway.

Only for a moment did Philippe stand still. Then he gathered his wits together. Off he dashed, after Zelie and Tom. But even though Philippe had followed almost immediately, they had now completely disappeared.

Thinking that he had been mistaken in the direction, Philippe turned around quickly and started down another street. Oh, he must find Zelie and Tom. He had missed them so. He wanted to talk with them again.

Frantically he turned, and once more he ran down the alleyway. There was a group of children playing on the curb.

"Have you seen a man and a girl with an organ?" asked Philippe in French.

The children did not understand. They giggled. Philippe realized that in Antwerp most of the people speak Flemish. He repeated his question in that language.

"Yes," replied one of the children. "They went very fast down that way. They went past the church toward the station."

Calling back his thanks, Philippe darted off in the direction given. Asking questions as he went, he finally arrived at the railway station. Puffing and panting, he dashed up to the station master.

"Have you seen—a tall man—and a girl—with an organ?" puffed Philippe.

The station master smiled at the wild face of the boy before him.

Then he pointed to a train just chugging away and replied, "They are on that train which is leaving the station."

Philippe's face fell. His heart pounded.

"Where is that train going?" he demanded.

"To Ghent," replied the station master, smiling. "It is too late to catch it now."

"When does the next train leave for Ghent?" asked Philippe.

"There is no train for Ghent tonight—only a freight train which leaves here in an hour," the man answered.

The boy thanked the station master and turned away quickly. Philippe knew that he would not be allowed to ride on the freight train. But he also knew that he was going to follow his friends to Ghent if he had to board the train secretly and hide.

And that is just what he did. A wild idea had come into his head. Why should he go back to Brussels with the two gentlemen? Why should he begin all over again that dull life in the market place? Why not run away and join Tom and Zelie? They were not far. They were in Ghent. Yes, Philippe would go to Ghent.

So, huddled between boxes and crates, the boy and his puppy sat still in the stuffy freight car and waited for it to leave the station. Finally it pulled out, and Philippe knew that he was on his way to Ghent and to his friends.

Then he began to think of the thing he had done. What would the two foreign gentlemen think? What would his father and mother do when the gentlemen returned to Brussels without their boy?

Philippe smiled to himself as he thought, "I shall write to them. They will be pleased when I send them great sums of money."

Poor Philippe! Little did he know what awaited him! Little did he dream that much trouble lay between himself and his return home.

He only knew that at last he was off on his adventure. Young Philippe was now going forth into the world like a knight of old. But instead of riding a steed, this knight sat huddled in an old freight car with a fat puppy in his arms.

Chapter VIII

A DIFFICULT JOURNEY

Belgium has more miles of railway than any other country of its size in the world.

Philippe was having a noisy ride, huddled up in the corner of a freight car. He was tired out from all the excitement of travel during the day. Even the sounds of passing trains, the swaying motion, the puff-puffing and shrill whistling all around him could not keep him awake. Philippe and Trompke slept.

Philippe did not know how long he had been sleeping when he suddenly sat up straight. The train had stopped. The boy rubbed his eyes. All was black around him. He could feel the soft coat of Trompke beside him.

He felt for the door of the car and opened it. Then he jumped out, followed by Trompke. He found himself standing beside the freight car. It was night. They were in the middle of a field, far out in the country. The rest of the train had, no doubt, gone off and left them behind.

He was alone. Probably the rest of the freight train was now in Ghent. But his car had been left in this deserted place for some reason which Philippe did not know.

He started across the field toward a farmhouse. He was very hungry! If only he might go in and ask for something to eat. But it was very late at night. The people were surely asleep, and he must not awaken them.

There was a barn near the house. Philippe decided to sleep there. He could go to the house in the morning and ask for food. So he climbed up into a hay loft. The hay was soft and sweet; snuggling down, the boy and the dog were soon asleep. It must have been nearly dawn, when Philippe was awakened by voices below him. Not stirring, he listened. He heard two men, who had entered and were unharnessing a horse.

"It was the best fair of the year," said one.

In Belgium there are many fairs all the year round.

"Ah, ho, hum!" yawned the other man. "But we stayed in Ghent so long! Now we shall have only a short time to sleep before starting the day's work."

"Never mind," the other man declared, "it was worth the drive. And besides, the fair is leaving Ghent tomorrow."

Philippe put his chin on his elbow and listened. Then the man began to sing:

"I wouldn't be a lettuce

With my head all thrown about."

"That was the song that the gypsy girl sang; wasn't it?" asked the other.

"Yes," replied the first.

Philippe could hardly believe what he heard. That was his song! He had taught that song to Rose! Zelie must be singing his songs at the fair in Ghent.

Philippe was about to call down to the men. Then he stopped. They might mistake him for a tramp. They might do him some harm. No; he must be careful.

Then, yawning sleepily, the two men stamped out of the barn. Philippe heard the door closing behind them.

The only sound now was the crunch-crunching of the horse. But even that did not remind Philippe of his hunger. He could think of only one thing. He must reach Ghent as quickly as possible! He must find his friends before they left. He must join them at the fair in Ghent.

Philippe rose and went down into the barn. The men had locked the door; but there was a tiny window above the horse's stall. Through this, the boy first pushed Trompke. Then he started to climb through it himself.

"Come, Trompke," he called. "We must walk to Ghent. There is no time to lose. We must get there before the fair moves on."

Dawn was in the sky as the boy and his dog trudged wearily along the road. They were in the famous flax-growing district of Belgium. There were many glistening canals and rows of tall trees. They crossed bridges and passed low farmhouses with red roofs. But not once did Philippe stop.

Though his legs ached, never once did the boy give in. Trompke's tongue swept the ground. He was too tired to bark even at birds and chickens.

They passed fields of flax. This flax is sent to the factories of Ghent where it is made into fine linen.

The word "Ghent" is taken from the French word "gant," meaning "glove." Ghent was once famous for glove making. But today the lace and linen trades are more popular.

At last Philippe could see the outline of houses in the distance. It was bright sunlight now. There was smoke curling up from chimneys. People were cooking breakfast in Ghent.

Philippe could not let himself think of that. To the market place he went.

"Where is the fair?" he asked a passerby.

"It left Ghent last night," was the answer. "It will be in Bruges (brōō'jez) for three days, and I only wish I could go there and see it again."

Philippe did not hear the last remark. He had already turned. Everything had begun to whirl about him. But he stumbled on, on.

"We must follow them to Bruges, Trompke," he said, bravely.

But Trompke lay down on the sidewalk with his head between his paws. His tongue was lolling. His eyes said, "Not I! I stay!"

But Philippe was already walking away. Trompke arose wearily and followed. What dog has the right to refuse the commands of a boy? It is true that in this case the dog was more sensible than the boy.

For Philippe was completely worn out. He was so tired and hungry, he could scarcely think. It would have been better had he rested awhile.

But all he could think of was finding Tom and Zelie and joining them.

Chapter IX

THE CITY OF SISTERS

Philippe approached the great Convent of Ghent. This convent is different from most convents. It is like a little village where each sister has her own cosy house. These sisters have given up the life of the world. They live their own lives in this City of Sisters. They spend their time making beautiful laces, doing charity work and going to church.

Philippe had heard of the convent in Ghent. He had seen some of the sisters in Brussels at times. He knew they were kind and he determined to enter one of their homes and ask for food.

At the gate of the convent, Philippe met an elderly sister. She wore a long black gown and a snow-white cap. Her face was ruddy and wrinkled. She smiled at Philippe and stopped.

"You look tired, little one," she said.

Philippe answered, "I have walked many miles. I am hungry."

The sister then led him into her wee house. It looked like a gingerbread house. It was like all the other houses at the convent. It was made of brick.

"Come, let me give you some broth," said the sister kindly.

And she gave Philippe a bowl of delicious broth. They sat together in her neat little room.

When Philippe finished the broth he said, "Thank you, my sister. You are very kind." Then he told her his story.

"I must go on to Bruges," he finished "For the fair is in Bruges, and I shall find my friends there."

The sister looked serious.

"My boy, does your mother know what you are doing?" she asked.

Philippe shook his head slowly and said, "But I shall write to her now if you will please give me a pen and some paper."

After he had written to his parents, the boy looked up and found the good sister's gaze upon him.

"Why don't you give up this idea and go home?" she asked.

But Philippe laughed.

"Oh, no," he replied, "I could not do that now. Why, Tom says I shall make great sums of money! Tom is a fine fellow! Oh, my parents will be glad that I went, when I make them rich."

But still the sister seemed worried.

"Stay with me a day or so," she urged. "You are worn out with your long walk. Let me give you rest and food. Then perhaps we may find a way to send you to Bruges."

Philippe patted her rough, capable hand.

"Thank you, my sister," he said, "but I must waste no time."

Then the sister arose and went to a little table. She took from a drawer a linen bag. From the bag she brought forth some money.

Handing it to Philippe, she said, "Take this, little one, and ride to Bruges on it. That way you will reach your friends quickly and save your strength."

Philippe hesitated at first.

Then he took the money and said, "I can never thank you enough. But I shall return this money to you. You shall see."

After Philippe had washed and prepared to leave, he said to his new friend, "I have heard so much about the fine lace which is made by the sisters of the convent. May I see some of it?"

The good woman smiled and led the boy to another room to show him her work.

But suddenly Philippe started and looked about him with troubled eyes.

"My sister!" he cried, "I had a little dog. I almost forgot about him!"

"I saw your little dog," the sister answered. "He came in with you. But now he has disappeared."

Philippe began calling, "Trompke! Trompke!"

The sister helped him search the house.

"I cannot imagine where he went," exclaimed the sister.

Then they saw a strange sight.

From the big workbasket, where the sister kept her lace, came Trompke. He was completely wrapped in beautiful lace. He looked like a bride. His train was long and flowing. Upon his head was a lace cap. His dog face peered forth anxiously.

His tail stirred the lace train as it wagged, as if it were asking, "Were you looking for me?" For, you know, dogs speak with their tails.

Trompke waddled up to Philippe and continued to talk in tail language as if he were saying, "I was fast asleep in the workbasket. I was very tired. The lace was soft."

As soon as Philippe recovered from his amazement, he fell on his knees and began to untangle the lace from the dog's body.

"Oh, Trompke! Shame, Trompke!" he cried.

But the sister was laughing so hard that her kind, red face grew even redder than usual.

"Do not scold him," she said, "He did no harm. Oh, what a funny sight!"

And again the good sister went into peals of laughter. Her mirth started Philippe to thinking. A plan was forming in his mind.

Suddenly he jumped to his feet and exclaimed, "My sister, I have thought of a plan!"

The sister wiped the tears of laughter from her eyes. She listened to the boy.

"It suddenly came to me as you were laughing," he said, "that if the sight of Trompke seemed so funny to you, why would it not be funny to others?"

The sister gave signs of exploding again at the mention of lace-gowned Trompke.

But Philippe went on, "Give me some of your lace. I will dress Trompke as a bride in the market place of Bruges. People will stop. And when they stop, I shall sell them your lace. I shall be able, then, to repay you."

The sister looked into Philippe's eyes. She seemed much interested in what he had said.

She replied, "You have thought of a very clever plan. You are one who will make much of your life. That is plain to see."

Without wasting any time, the sister and Philippe prepared for the boy's journey.

Soon Philippe was leaving the tiny house with a bundle of lace tucked under his arm. His good friend walked with him as far as the gates of the convent.

As Philippe looked back, he saw the sister standing at the big iron gates, waving to him.

She looked after him and thought, "What a clever little fellow he is!"

She did not know what a disobedient little fellow Philippe really was. Also, she did not know that she was sending him to a thief. But then, neither did Philippe know this. He had told her that Tom and Zelie were his friends and that they were fine people. Philippe honestly believed this.

As he walked, he turned every little while to wave back to the sister. At last the City of Sisters faded from sight.

Chapter X

IN THE SHADOWS OF BRUGES

Philippe traveled comfortably to Bruges. Thanks to his friend, the sister, he rode in a train. He left the glass-roofed station of Ghent, and soon the train was speeding through flat, fertile country. It was not long before the old city of Bruges loomed into sight.

The word "Bruges" means "Bridges," and it is no wonder that the city bears that name. For everywhere one looks, one sees a bridge.

Bruges is a very old city. Once, long years ago, it was a famous port. Fabrics of many kinds came into Bruges. Famous Belgian laces and linens were shipped from there to other countries.

But since the discovery of America, Bruges has been very quiet. For with the discovery of the new world came a great change. There came new methods of trading. Bruges sank back upon her bridges and let the rest of the world go by.

Philippe sat in his railway coach. He looked out of the window and thought how very gray and dull the old city looked.

"I should not like to be alone on those old cobbled streets at night," he shivered.

The tall steeples of the old churches threw shadows. Ghosts of knights in armor might well prowl those streets! Again Philippe shuddered.

He began to be a little homesick. He began to think about his mother and Papa Pomme and Baby Rose. He had disobeyed his parents. He had left those two kind gentlemen without saying a word.

What would they think of him? Philippe knew that he had done wrong. But somehow he knew that he was going to keep right on until he found Tom and Zelie. He could not give up now.

The train pulled into the station and stopped. The boy started out in search of the fair. To the market place he went. Crowds were there. It was a gay sight. Booths were everywhere. There were merry-go-rounds and swinging boats and shooting galleries and candy stands.

Children were all about, laughing, singing, eating. Philippe's eye was trained, and he knew market places. He had spent most of his life in one. So he found a spot for himself and began to dress the dog, Trompke.

Trompke disapproved. But Philippe won the battle, and soon the dog was dressed in lace cap and veil. His worried, wrinkled face looked out from under the dainty lace cap. His tail wiggled the handsome lacy train.

Philippe sang to attract the crowds and soon people began to stop and to laugh at Trompke. All the time Philippe was looking about him, while his heart beat fast.

Perhaps a few feet away from him were his friends. He hoped that he would find them. Perhaps Zelie had sung to the same people who were now laughing at Trompke.

The boy examined every booth. But there was no sign of Tom or Zelie.

Meanwhile the sister's lace was selling fast. People stopped to laugh and to pet Trompke. The little boy explained to them about the lace.

"The finest lace in all the world, madam," said he, "made by the sisters in Ghent. A very excellent bargain."

Philippe sold all his lace and found his pockets bulging with money. How pleased the good sister would be!

Besides, he had made extra money for himself. People gave him extra money because they liked his sweet voice and because Trompke made them laugh.

But the heart of Philippe was heavy. He had not seen Tom and Zelie! He was in a strange city; he was far from home, and it was growing late.

Philippe now walked slowly to the post office. Here he sent away two letters. One was to his father.

He told his father not to worry about him. He said that he could not return to Brussels because he was going to make his way and send them a great deal of money. He enclosed some bills in the envelope, and he felt proud.

The other letter was to the sister and contained the money in payment for the laces and also payment of the amount the sister had loaned him.

He still had money in his pocket. He bought food. But Trompke ate most of it. Somehow Philippe did not feel hungry. He was too excited.

Chapter XI

FOUND

The shadows were falling in Bruges. The high towers were reflected in the canals. The city was slowly being covered by night.

A terrible, lonesome feeling came over Philippe as he watched the darkness stealing on. How could he stay all night in the ghostly darkness of this old city? His teeth began to chatter.

A boy about his own age came up to him.

"Where are you going?" asked the boy.

"I don't know," answered Philippe truthfully.

"You don't know?" the boy laughed. "Then let me take you somewhere. Have you some money?"

Philippe showed the stranger his money.

"We can go to the cinema," smiled the boy eagerly.

So Philippe was taken to a theater by his new companion. Philippe was tired and discouraged and sank down in his seat with a sigh. He wanted to go home.

He was afraid of the dark city and the strange shadows. He knew he had done wrong. Now he was ready to give up.

But as he watched the flickering shadow people on the screen, he thought of that other film which he had seen with his father. He remembered the brave Belgian soldiers and the heroic King Albert. Then he had wanted to be a hero, too. But now he was acting like a coward.

This film story was a romance with knights on fiery steeds. What adventure those brave knights had! They did not give up and go home. They came home in glory and each married a princess!

Philippe sat up straight. He saw himself as one of those knights. Then he turned suddenly to the boy next to him.

"Did you see a man and a girl with an organ today at the fair?" he asked.

"Yes," replied the boy at his side, "They were at the fair, and the girl sang."

"Did you notice which way they went when they left the market place?" Philippe demanded quickly.

"Well— " hesitated the other, "I did see them going down—Oh, don't bother me now. I want to see the film," he added irritably.

But Philippe had him by the shoulders.

"Come out of here," he ordered.

The boy was too amazed to refuse. Together the two marched out of the theater.

On the sidewalk Philippe seized the boy's arm and said to him, "I must find those people. Do you understand? Now, you've got to think which way you saw them go!"

After Philippe had told his story and explained about Tom and Zelie, the other boy remarked, "Well, my friends and I followed the organ man to a narrow little street where the poorest people live. The place was very dark, even in the daytime. It frightened some of the little children; so we left. We did not stay to see where the organ man went."

Philippe thanked his new acquaintance, and the boy was glad to go back to his seat in the theater.

Philippe followed directions, and soon he was in the dingy little street in which Tom and Zelie had disappeared.

No one was about. It was the blackest, most silent place Philippe had ever been in. He and his dog huddled beside a wall. There was nobody whom he could ask for information. Had he the courage to ring a doorbell?

He started toward a door. His finger was about to push the bell when a voice called to him. The voice came from above.

Philippe looked up, and there was Tom!

He was looking out of a window. It was so dark that Philippe could not see Tom's face very clearly. But his voice was cheery.

"Hello, my lad," he called. "So you've come to us at last!"

Philippe ran up the steps, and Tom let him into the house. It was a poor house and smelled musty and old.

Tom was very pleased to see the boy.

"I knew that some day you would come," he said, slapping Philippe on the back. "You are a fine brave lad, and we shall have a splendid life together, wandering on the road."

"Where is Zelie?" asked Philippe.

"Ah, she will soon be home. She is so busy. She works very late sometimes," answered Tom smiling.

"What does she do?" Philippe asked after a little silence.

"She plays the organ, and she sings," the man replied. "Now, you shall join her, and together you two should bring in much money."

His eyes gleamed. Philippe did not feel very happy. But he could not tell why. Perhaps he was just tired, and tomorrow all would be well.

Then suddenly from the street below, there came a howl. Philippe ran to the window and saw his dog, Trompke, below. The fat puppy was whimpering and calling his master. He had been forgotten outside.

Philippe smiled at Tom.

"That is my Trompke," he said.

They opened the door, and the puppy flew up the steps into Philippe's arms. Philippe stroked him, and then he told Tom how Trompke had helped him to sell the sister's lace. Tom was delighted.

"What a bright boy you are!" he exclaimed. "You shall continue selling lace for me. That is a splendid plan."

Just then Zelie came home. She seemed thinner and paler than when Philippe had last seen her. She did not talk very much, but her face lit up when she saw Philippe.

"I am so glad you have come," she said. "We shall have such good times together."

Tom grinned broadly.

"Yes, indeed," he agreed. "There is a fair in Ostend (ŏst-ĕnd'), so we four shall start our wanderings tomorrow."

"We four?" asked Zelie.

She had not noticed Trompke. The puppy was curled up behind a chair.

"Yes," smiled Tom slyly. "The little dog is to be one of our party, and a very important one, too. Eh, Philippe, my boy?"

Philippe smiled and began to feel happier. At last he was going to do the thing he had always dreamed of doing. At last he was going to travel with Tom and Zelie.

Chapter XII

PHILIPPE FINDS OUT

So Tom went out next day and purchased some lace at a very cheap price. He and the two children packed their things, and started on their journey.

Philippe's plan succeeded, and Tom was delighted with the way the lace-gowned dog drew the crowds. Philippe and Zelie sang together, and people thought the two children very attractive. They brought in much money for Tom.

From town to town they traveled.

Tom always seemed gay and pleasant. The only times he ever showed his ill nature was when the children did not bring in enough money. Then his scowls were very disagreeable to see. But usually he was pleased with what Philippe and Zelie and Trompke made.

They arrived at the fair in Ostend, a famous beach resort of Belgium. They attracted the attention of many children along the wide beach. Here they saw hundreds of bathing machines.

These machines are little houses on wheels, in which people dress and undress. Horses are hitched to the houses. They pull them to the water's edge, where the bathers jump into the sea for their swim.

From Ostend they journeyed to Courtrai (kōō-trĕ') and the flax fields.

Philippe noticed how much the Belgian people living near the border of France resemble the French people.

In sections of Belgium close to Holland, the people wear wooden shoes and look very Dutch. Their language, Flemish, is indeed almost the same as the Dutch language.

As they wandered through the Belgian villages the smell of cows and fresh hay greeted their nostrils.

Nearly everyone is poor in these villages. The women wear bedroom slippers in the street.

They now came to Tournai (toor-nĕ'), which is one of the most ancient towns in Belgium. It dates from the time of Julius Caesar.

As they approached the city of Mons, (môns) they passed great coal mines. These mines were taken over by the Germans during the World War.

While armies were fighting in France and destroying French property, Belgian farms and factories were being well run by the Germans. That is why our travelers, wandering over the country of Belgium, saw few ruins.

They trudged along black roads and passed great chimney stacks.

Several times Philippe had sent money home to his parents.

But one day Tom said, "I must ask you to give me all the money you make. It is I who feed and clothe you. And now you belong to me."

Philippe had a strange feeling then.

He answered, "But I must send my parents some of what I make. It is only fair."

Tom scowled fearfully and snapped, "You will do as I say!"

After that time Philippe worried. He told Zelie, but she said nothing. She looked very sad, however.

Then one evening while they were having supper by the side of the road, Tom announced, "It is time that Philippe learned our business, eh, Zelie?"

Zelie started and turned very pale, but she did not answer.

"Listen," continued Tom. He leaned over toward Philippe. "Do you see that farm over there?"

He pointed to a little peaceful-looking farm in the distance. Philippe nodded. He wondered what Tom was going to say. Tom had never talked like this before.

"Tonight we shall go to that farm," Tom went on, "and we shall take a wheelbarrow along, and we shall help ourselves to all the fine vegetables there. Tomorrow we shall set up in the market place. You have sold vegetables in market places before, eh, my Philippe?"

But the boy could not answer. He was horrified.

It all came to him then. This was the vegetable thief—the man who had stolen his own father's vegetables! Tom! Oh, what a foolish boy he had been! Why hadn't he listened to his parents? He was traveling with a thief!

Tom said in an irritable voice, "Come on, boy! Don't stare at me like that! Wake up, and we shall teach you!"

But Philippe had jumped up quickly and stood before Tom. His fists were clenched and his cheeks burned.

"No, no! I won't steal," he cried. "It is wicked to steal! I will not help you!"

Tom only smiled calmly.

Then he said, "Oh, very well, my boy. Do not excite yourself. You need not come along, since you feel that way. Zelie and I have always done well. We can still get along without you. You shall do your work by singing, and we by stealing. That is simple."

But Philippe was angry.

"Oh, you wicked man!" he cried. "I will not stay with you any longer. I am going home!"

Then Tom caught hold of the boy's arm. Tom's eyes flashed.

"No!" he said firmly, "No. You had better not try that. You are mine, and you shall stay with me!"

That night Tom locked Philippe in the room of a little hotel while he and Zelie went to the farm.

Philippe wrote a letter to his father. He told all of what had happened. He begged forgiveness and asked his father to come and get him.

But when Tom returned, he found the letter and burned it.

"Do not try any tricks," he said, "for you will be sorry."

He yawned sleepily and went to bed.

When Philippe heard Tom's snores, he tried to run away. But Zelie stopped him at the door.

"Don't go," she said. "Please don't go. He will find you, and then he will beat you."

"How do you know?" asked Philippe.

"Because," Zelie replied, "he has done it to me!"

And then Philippe knew why Zelie's eyes were so sad and held a look of fear.

"Oh, Zelie," Philippe cried, "I am so sorry for you. You are so brave."

Zelie then began to cry softly.

"Sometimes I am very sad," she sobbed. "That is why I was so glad to see you. Before you came, oh, he made me work so hard!"

"Do not cry, Zelie," said Philippe, "but tell me all about it. I will protect you."

Philippe suddenly felt very brave. He felt like one of those knights he had seen in the film. He felt like a hero out of a fairy tale. He knew that he was only a boy, but he had great courage, and he wanted to protect Zelie.

"We two will escape," he promised the girl. "You'll see. Now tell me everything."

Then Zelie told Philippe that Tom was not really her father.

"My mother and father died when I was a baby," she told him, "and this man is my uncle. Oh, he is a very bad man, and he has made me steal, and if he ever should catch us trying to escape—oh, oh!"

The poor little girl again began to sob.

"Stop, Zelie," urged Philippe. "I have a plan, and we will escape."

Zelie dried her eyes. Then she went to her room, and Philippe started to think.

Chapter XIII

THE CAVE OF THE CROWS

Philippe tried several times after that to post a letter. But Tom's eyes were very keen, and he seemed to see everything at once.

Ever since that day, Tom had watched Philippe all the time. But the man acted no differently than before. He whistled a great deal and was pleased with the money that the children brought in.

Still he worked them harder than ever. Often Philippe's legs ached with standing so long. Often his throat was sore with singing.

He knew that he was being punished for his disobedience. He knew that if he ever escaped from this wicked man he would always obey his parents.

Tom often joked with Philippe, and the boy told him stories about the country through which they traveled. But all the while, Tom did not know what plans were shaping in Philippe's head.

One day as they tramped along, Philippe carried a letter in his pocket. The letter was to Papa Pomme. Philippe was planning to post the letter when they reached Charleroi (shär-le-roi'), in the evening.

In it he told Papa Pomme everything. But he told him not to worry, that he was well, and also that he was laying a plan to capture the thief.

Part of Philippe's letter read: "I shall try to make him spend Monday night in the Cave of the Crows. That is the big rock between Namur (nâ-mür') and Dinant (dē-nän'). Send some one to that place, for if my plan succeeds we shall be there."

The Cave of the Crows is a mysterious rock out on the open road. There is a folk tale connected with it, and part of Philippe's plan was to tell this tale to Tom.

As they walked along, the boy kept thinking over his plan.

"If only I can persuade him to spend Monday night there!" Philippe mused earnestly.

They reached Charleroi, after passing the country of the iron workers.

Philippe found this part of the country different from that around Antwerp and Brussels. To him even the people seemed different. Here he found pine and birch trees and little stone houses.

Most of the people in northern Belgium are blond and large. Here they are dark and smaller and more lively.

Once in Charleroi, Philippe explained to Zelie what he wanted her to do. Zelie agreed to follow out the plan, and Philippe gave her the letter.

Then Philippe started to run down the street.

Zelie cried out to Tom, "Look! Quick! Philippe is running away!"

Tom was after the boy in a second, and Zelie quickly slipped Philippe's letter to Papa Pomme into the mail box.

But poor Philippe had to pay for this trick. Tom locked him up all day and gave him only bread and water.

Yet the boy's heart leaped with joy. Now the letter was off. It only remained for him to persuade Tom to spend the night in the cave.

It was pleasant country through which they were passing. Along the banks of the Sambre (sän'-br) River, they saw many women washing clothes. Men on barges waved and called to them. These men seemed a happy lot. Old castles loomed up.

Monday arrived. The three travelers were nearing the Cave of the Crows.

"Have you ever heard the story of the Cave of the Crows, sir?" asked Philippe.

"No," replied Tom. "Tell it to me."

He liked Philippe's stories. The little fellow had entertained him with many.

"They say," began Philippe, "that long, long years ago a wandering poet passed this cave, and there he met a beautiful fairy. He fell in love with her and she with him. They married and lived in the cave together.

"But one day the fairy was called to a gathering in fairyland. The other fairies were angry to learn that she had married a mortal. As a punishment the poor fairy was changed into an ugly black crow with a hoarse, terrible voice.

"She returned to the cave to her poet and found him also changed into a crow. But this did not spoil their love for each other. They lived happily in the cave for years and years, and they had many children. There are thousands of black crows flying about the cave, shrieking and cawing. These are the descendants of the poet and the poor fairy."

Tom shuddered.

"A very good place from which to keep away!" he laughed.

"Oh, no," replied Philippe. "On the contrary, I should like to go there. I should like to go," he added mysteriously, "because it is said that whoever spends a night in the cave will find a bag of gold in the morning."

Tom's eyes sparkled. Philippe's heart beat quickly.

He continued, "Yes, it is believed that robbers once buried a bag of gold in the cave. Anyone who is brave enough to spend a night there may have it."

Tom smiled, but looked doubtful.

"Let us go there, sir," suggested Philippe. "In the morning you shall find that bag of gold."

Tom thought awhile but did not reply. The boy nearly cried out in eagerness. Oh, if only the man would consent to do this thing!

The letter he had written to his father would reach Brussels today. His father would send some one to the cave tonight. Then he and Zelie would be free, and Tom captured.

What had Papa Pomme said? Oh, yes! The thief must go to prison!

Suddenly Tom spoke. "No," he said. "I think we shall move on. It might be dangerous to stay in that cave."

"What!" cried Philippe. "Are you afraid of the crying of crows?"

"No," replied the man, "It is not that. I prefer to spend my nights in cities."

Philippe's heart sank.

"But, sir," he said, "would you let such a chance of gaining wealth escape you? They say that the bag of gold is very large indeed!"

"Then why is it that no one has ever found it before?" asked Tom suspiciously.

"Because," answered Philippe, "there is no one with courage enough. One must be brave to spend a night in such a cold, dark place with howling birds all about. That requires courage like yours, sir!"

The man was pleased with the boy's flattery.

"Do you really think that the bag of gold is worth the trouble?" he asked.

"Worth it!" exclaimed Philippe. "Why, sir, it will make you rich!"

Now, Tom, like most wicked men, was ignorant. He had never gone to school and he could not even read. Though he was sharp and quick, he had no learning and he was not very shrewd. He believed the boy's story.

Philippe had seemed to know a great deal about the country. The lad had told many true stories. He had shown his knowledge on any number of occasions. Besides, Tom was so greedy that he could not bear to let a chance like this go by.

Of course, Tom knew that this was only a belief. But then, there had been robbers everywhere at one time, and they might easily have buried their treasure in this mysterious cave.

"Very well," he said, "we shall spend the night in the Cave of the Crows!"

Chapter XIV

TROMPKE TALKS

It was a weird place to which Philippe led his little party. Crows, descendants of the poet and the fairy, flew all about. The noise they made was deafening.

Philippe was in a state of great excitement; and the screeching and yelling of the thousands of birds made his head whirl.

As night came, however, the crows grew quieter. The little group settled itself to rest.

The man said, "This is your doing, boy. If there is no bag of gold in the morning I shall make your head feel like a bag of gold!"

He smiled, but Philippe saw a wicked gleam in his eye.

They were all tired, and soon Tom fell asleep; but not Philippe and Zelie! The boy and girl lay awake and stared into the darkness. They listened. They waited.

Now, if only some one would come! This was their one chance to capture Tom and to free themselves. The night wore on. But no one came.

Philippe could stand it no longer. What if Papa Pomme had not received his letter?

The boy stirred slowly and sat up. Suppose morning came and no one arrived? Tom would not find a bag of gold, and he would surely beat poor Philippe for deceiving him.

No, he could not take that chance. There was only one thing to do. He must try to escape with Zelie now.

Philippe stole softly to his little friend's side.

"Quiet, quiet, Zelie! Not a sound! Come with me," he whispered.

Softly, silently they tiptoed toward the entrance of the cave.

But Philippe had forgotten one thing. He had forgotten Trompke. And Trompke was not to be forgotten! The little dog lay chained to a rock.

Tom always took care to keep him tied. Trompke was an important member of that little group.

As the boy and girl neared the door, Trompke awoke. Dogs do not sleep as soundly as people. Trompke's brow wrinkled. He cocked his puzzled head on one side. His tail began to speak.

"Where are you going, my little master?" asked Trompke's tail.

But the children were at the door. They did not hear the tail language.

So Trompke had to use his mouth. He barked. He barked again.

Philippe clutched Zelie's hand and ran out of the cave.

But the first bark had awakened Tom. He was up like a jack rabbit. He cried out to them to stop. But they kept on running.

Tom was swift, and it was not long before he overtook them. Back to the cave he brought them. Philippe could see that he was very angry.

"Make ready to leave," he commanded Zelie.

Morning was in the sky now. Tom stood before Philippe, and his eyes flashed. But Philippe's eyes were steady.

"You are brave, eh?" sneered Tom. "Only brave men will spend a night in the cave. Well, my hero, where is the gold?"

Philippe answered, "I do not know, sir."

"Tricks!" roared Tom.

Then he took a stick.

Meanwhile a big touring car was driving along the road toward the cave. It was the car belonging to the two gentlemen who had taken Philippe to Antwerp.

When Papa Pomme had received the letter from Philippe he had immediately shown it to the gentlemen. They had been terribly worried about the boy and had tried in every way to help the poor parents.

When the two gentlemen read of Philippe's plan to capture Tom at the cave, they immediately told the police. Soon the big touring car with the two gentlemen and two policemen was on its way to the cave.

"This is the place," cried one of the officers.

The car stopped. The four men jumped out. With their guns drawn, they entered the cave.

They heard Tom laughing and saying, "Now, after I have beaten you, perhaps you will not try any more tricks. We shall leave for other lands, where you cannot escape so easily. We shall go to France and England and then— —"

Suddenly Tom stopped speaking. His jaw dropped open. The stick fell from his hands. He saw a sight that made him turn pale. For two gentlemen and two policemen stood in the door of the cave. Each policeman was pointing a pistol at Tom!

Then the Englishman and the American walked over to them.

"The plans for your trip sound very interesting," said the Englishman in French to Tom. "But I am afraid we must spoil them. There is another trip which we have planned for you, instead."

The American looked very thoughtful.

"How in the world do you say 'prison' in French?" he asked.

"The same as in English," answered his friend.

They marched outside to the car. Tom was handcuffed. He walked between two policemen. Zelie walked with Philippe. They entered the big car and started off. Tom was scowling fiercely.

The American smiled and said, "In our country the children sing this song." He sang:

"Off to prison you must go,

You must go,

You must go,

Off to prison you must go,

My fair lady!"

Philippe echoed, "My fair leddy!"

Together they repeated the song, Zelie joining in. Philippe did not understand what he was singing. He did not care, for he was very happy.

The road ran along the beautiful River Meuse (mūz). Philippe watched the patient fishermen sitting on the banks. "How peaceful and quiet it is to stay at home!" he thought.

Chapter XV

A NEW SONG

The two gentlemen have gone back to their respective countries.

Now once again Philippe and Rose sit in the market place of Brussels.

Once again the little boy sells his mother's vegetables, while the pretty baby sings to the passers-by.

There is also another child. That other is Zelie, who now lives with them. There is no more sadness in her eyes now.

But Philippe has changed. He has at last had the adventures about which he has read and dreamed so much. And he is glad that they are over.

The Belgian people say that there is no place like home, and Philippe now agrees with them.

He has made up a new song. He has used the old Belgian saying, "East, west, home's best," for that song. Listen! Philippe and Rose and Zelie are singing it now:

"Winds blow,

Rivers flow,

Time flies and days go.

Storms sweep,

Shadows creep,

Stars shoot and fires leap.

Things sprout

All about,

Folks dash in and out.

Roads wind,

Leave behind

Us three, peace to find.
Philippe will
Sit still;
Never more seek a thrill.
Zelie knows,
So does Rose,
Philippe would rather doze
In a nook
With a book;
Some day be a cook.
All may go
To and fro,
Here, there, high and low,
But we rest
In our nest,
For east, west, home's best!"